POLYNESIA BEGINS

POLYNESIA BEGINS

D. B. CLARK

EDITED BY CAROL CLARK

POLYNESIA BEGINS

iUniverse books may be ordered through booksellers or by contacting:

iUniverse
1663 Liberty Drive
Bloomington, IN 47403
www.iuniverse.com
844-349-9409

ISBN: 978-1-6632-0858-3 (sc)
ISBN: 978-1-6632-0859-0 (e)

Print information available on the last page.

iUniverse rev. date: 09/21/2020

Current Polynesia is totally ethnically diverse. Every race on Earth is represented in the total Pacific expanse. In the two or so years of Colonial occupation, Polynesia was less diverse. Some authorities speculate that white Aryans might have been a part of the mix, along with so-called yellow Chinese, and brown Southern Asians.

But in know prehistory, this racial mixture ended up in New Zealand. And it from there that Kermicha's people moved to Kermadec Island, and this totally fictional story begins. So, think of Kermicha's people as living in a time when only that reduced number of ethnic people, who ended up on New Zealand existed, and no people existed on any of the multitude of Pacific islands from Kermadec Island to Hawaii.

And furthermore, the language, the culture, the religion, and the mythology of Kermicha's people comes only from this author's mind. But, I do hope it is enchanting enough to maintain your attention. If not, blame it on me, not on Kermicha.

KERMACHA'S POLYNESIA BEGINS

Mother Mancha whispered to herself, "Kermie, my child, as I observe you now, as a three year old, I recall this poem I wrote for you:

> *Kermie, my, precious child,*
>
> *Mother Merciful, without pain,*
>
> *Bade thee arrive.*
>
> *So, now awake in wisdom for awhile.*
>
> *Then close again thy eyes.*

Then Kermie interrupted his mother's thinking, asking, "Mommy, where did I come from"

"From my belly, Kermie, dear. We've talked about this many times,"

"No, not that. I mean where did I from before I was in your belly?"

Mother Mancha laughed, "Now that's certainly a big boy question. You really are growing up fast. I guess, since you are such a good boy, you must have come from some holy place where strong boys like you are created to be sent forth to save us weaker people."

"Kermie laughed too, "Yeah, that's who I want to be. But, before I started to become that strong boy, where did I come from before you and I lived here on Kermadec Island?

"Now that is a question I can answer," Mother Mancha said. "We came from the beginning Island of New Zealand"

"The beginning Island? But there must have been another Island before that."

"Yes, my parents, and their parents, and their parents must have come from some land further Northwest, maybe."

Kermie paused for a moment, then said, "I guess I understand."

"Then you understand more than I do," said his mother.

"Well maybe. But this is what I believe. There is a place where we, came from, somewhere, which must have been a good place, because you and I have become good people. So, want you now what I want to know is, where am I going to go when I grow up and leave you?

Then Mother Mancha looked sad, sad like all mothers are when they must accept that a child must leave them. "Where do *you* want to go Kermie?" she whispered.

Kermie looked happy, no eager, and certainly not sad like his mother. Then he said firmly, I want to sail on a ship that I make, all by myself, to an even better land than where our family originally came from, even better than New Zealand, and to land where I can come back from to bring you, and Father, and all our people here on Kermadec Island!"

Kermie's mother looked no longer sad, but now immensely proud, "Yes, my darling Kermie. I know you will do just that!"

Kermie's Father Phachama recalled this poem he wrote for his son, after he had helped him build his boat:

Father Enabler, my son Kermie

Wants to sail the sea,

With only his wisdom and thee

To keep him company.

At least I will help him make this sturdy boat

That, in spite of the sea's treachery

Will remain afloat

And bring him safely back to me.

Now he watched Kermie set sail in the pond behind their small farm, and wondered what his adventurous son was thinking. Great deeds, no doubt.

Kermie sat in the seat in the middle of his new boat from which he could paddle on his own,. He had raised a palm branch for a sail, but he was mostly paddling, since there was little breeze in the pond behind his family's farm. Nevertheless, he was glad the little girl, whose name was Meacha, was watching from the other side of the pond.

She waved to him, but Kermie ignored her, not wanting her to think the this manly sailor could be interested in a mere girl.

But she was just as smart as Kermie, and she knew it.

Then, Kermacha forgot about Meacha. He was who he wanted to be. He was Kermacha, the great explorer, who was sailing far from Kermadec Island, outward over the endless, empty sea, to find the great new island where his people could live more freely than were now living on clouded Kermadec Island.

And if Meacha knew what he was planning, would she be frightened, or so proud she would want to go with him?

But little Kermie had a lot of growing up to do before he would become his fantasy heroic explorer.

Before a boy could become a man on Kermadec Island, he had to prove himself against like-age boys, in activities such as running, swimming, tree felling, spear throwing, and leadership. Those boys who failed more than one category, would have to try again next year.

Kermie was a likely winner in all categories, except perhaps for tree felling. In the category, his chief rival was Brutachar. Brutachar was slightly shorter than Kermie, but much wider, and obviously very strong. When Kermie had watched Brutacha chop down a portia tree, the tree seemed almost shattered. But Kermie reminded himself, that shattered trees were worthless. Portia trees were use in building sea ship, and needed to be strong and almost shatter proof. So, let Brutachar win this one.

Kermie had no trouble winning all other contests, although in spear throwing, it was a tossup. Brutachar could through longer, and Kermie could through more accurately. Leadership, however, was a different kind of skill, one that was to be judged by the elders after the observed the contestants interactions with one another. So, Kermie decided to not worry about leadership till later.

Kermie, with his long legs and deep breathing, from intense working sessions when helping father on the farm, was and easy winner in running.

And it was in swimming that Kermie would have no rivals. And here, the bulky Brutachar would be in great trouble. Afterall, the other contestants said, "Kermie was obviously a fish, and poor Brutachar was a clam that would sink to the bottom.

Kermie easily out sped all the other contestants, and was standing on the side of the dock, waiting for the other to join him.

But Brutarcha fail to rise to the surface!

All knew what had happened. Brutarchar must have sunk to the bottom. So, Kermie instantly jumped in, expecting to drag Brudarchar to the surface. But to Kermie's horror, Brutarchar was not on the bottom. *He was in the mouth of a giant squid!*

Kermie hoped that the large breath he had taken before jumping into the water would keep him conscious long enough to do what he planned. He swam around to the other side of the stretched out squid, and took out his knife, that he always carried with him, and began stabbing the Squid in its eye. After many stabs, the Squid opened his large mouth and belch out the squirming Brutarchar.

The giant squid was doing its own squirming as it swam away, and to Kermie's relief, ignore the rapidly surfacing Kermie.

The other contestants had dragged Brudarchar to the dock, and when Kermie reached him, he was already sitting up. He looked in pain, but not too damaged.

Kermie sighed his own relief, then started to walk away.

But Brudarchar would have now of that. He struggled to his feet, and rushed over to firstly hug Kermie, almost shouting, "Kermie, you will be my friend and leader for life. This is my pledge. I will follow you wherever you lead!"

Kermie freed himself from Brutarcha's embrace, and looked Brutarchar in the eyes, saying, "And I will accept that pledge, friend!"

Then Kermie also noticed that the elders had also noticed Brutarchar's pledge. I guess that answers the leadership question

Brutarchar and Kermie, now Kermicha, chopped down enough portia trees to build Kermicha's catamaran. Kermicha had warned his friend to chop lightly. He didn't want his catamaran to be shattered in the slightest breeze.

Brutarchar laughed, and the gently stroked the trunk of the portia tree they were chopping.

Then Kermicha's father joined the two in constructing Kermicha's single person catamaran. The work went quickly, though Brutarchar keep complaining that the boat should be a two-man catamaran.

On the morning of Kermicha's departure, his family, Brutachar, and Meacha were gathered on the dock, as were of the other residences of Keemadec Island. So, Kermicha decided it was time for him to honor these people with first poem. He stood tall on edge of the dock, his boat behind him, and tried to project his sometimes changing teenage voice to reach all the people.

Mother Merciful, protect me,
And Father Enabler make me brave
So I can overcome every ravaging wave,
As I sail into the unknown sea
To bring back to my people
Awareness of a new homeland
Where we will soon need to be.

The crowd was silent, except for a slight sigh from Kermicha's mother. Then Brutachar, first started clapping, and then cheering. Only then did the others join in.

But then, Kermicha noticed that the elders, the same elders who had instructed him in how to tack his craft back and forth, to maintain a steady heading. They had learned this from how the first Kermadec Islanders made their way to this island. Now, Kermicha guessed as they and all the other peered over Kermicha's shoulders, they saw only endless sea, and they had warned Kermicha and his family that their son would never return from that endless emptiness.

But Kermicha wasn't worried. He had faith in the feeling about what was beyond that emptiness.

Neither was his friend, Rrutachar worried. He was only annoyed that Kermicha wouldn't let him join him on this great adventure. But, at least Kermicha was going to let him join him until the boat was well away from the dock.

So, Kermacha, the great adventure, and his disappointed non-adventurer, set out to sea. And only when the boat reached swimming distance from the dock, did Kermicha insist the Brutachar beginning his swim back to the shore.

But he couldn't resist one last friendly jab at Brutachar, "Hey, friend, I noticed that our old buddy, the Brutarchar-chopping Squid had back near the dock."

Brutachar look downward briefly, a worried looking flashing across this face, than jumped into the water, *and swam very rapidly back to shore.*

And so, young Kermicha's journey to who knows where began. But the young adventurer, in his mind, knew where. It was to be a land that no one but he had ever seen, a land that once he had seen as a child, and somehow knew was there.

As Kermicha sailed along, not even needing to paddle, he felt confident that his long delayed journey was going to be smooth sailing.

Thank you, Father Enabler,

For caring for me.

I feel certain the that now,

Until journey's end,

I will be trouble free.

But after two days smooth sailing and restful sleep, when dark clouds and a quickening breeze, that turned into a wailing wind, Kermicha began to feel less confident. He whispered again to Father Enable, "Still be with me Father."

Father Enabler must have been listening. Kermicha instantly began tacking left and right, and he was thereby able to avoid what could have been a very rough ride.

He was still letting the wind steer his course, trusting his belief that Father Enable, and Mother Merciful believed that he was their favorite son . . . Well, maybe he was learning to navigate on his own, he though, trying to be at least a little modest.

And, feeling more mature, that next evening, before he fell asleep during a calm voyage, he allowed himself to fantasize about the other gods he had had experienced while still a child. When ever he misbehaved, which according to his mother was often, then Ante Switcher and Uncle Disabler would pop out of the closet and carry him off to their own cave-home, which wouldn't as pleasant as his home with Mother Mancha and Father Pachachama. That kept Kermie behaving, at least for awhile. Maybe it was his mother's small smile that kept Kermie from being completely good.

But the contained good weather gave Kermicha ample time to consider the way ahead. He moved to the front of his catamaran, so he could peer ahead. And he was rewarded with the site, in the distance, of another island.

Without even thinking, he let his imagination name the island, Tonga. And as he began paddling near shore, he could see there were amble portia trees, which seemed to be ficus-like, and could be used to make catamarans for transporting the Kermadec Islanders when Kermicha brought them to their new homeland . . . wherever that was going to be.

Relived, Kermicha settled down for a good night's sleep . . . only to have it interrupted by a dream . . . *no, a nightmare!*

He was about to be bitten by giant cobra, its swishing tongue licking toward him between giant fangs.

What was worse, the monster was laughing and *taking to him!*

"Of course, I'm talking to you, little boy Kermicha. I want you to know how much my venom is going to make you feel pain for daring to believe you, little boy, could find a land where you could lead your people. Foolish little boy. There is no such place! And your people wouldn't follow a little boy like you anyway."

Kermicha took in a deep breath, and then dared to move closer to the giant cobra . . . which started to grow smaller. "Look, little cobra, I am Kermicha, the fearless adventurer, and I *will* lead my people to their new homeland, which *does* exist"

Then the diminished cobra shrunk into a tiny hole in the ground.

Then Kermicha woke up, smiling . . . but he realized, sweating profusely . . . even though he was a little chilly.

Kermicha felt refreshed the next morning. It helped that he ate some roasted fish he had snagged while sailing. That, plus the fruit and nuts he pick from the trees on his Tonga Island, made him a little reluctant to set sail again, when he would have only raw food to eat.

But, now thinking of himself as an experienced sailor, he remembered to fill up his two jugs with fresh stream water.

But where next to head? Was it just pure luck that he had come upon such a refurbishing island, or had Father Enabler been guiding him.

Either way he patted his full belly, and thanked Mother Merciful profusely.

But now, being this experienced sailor, he would have himself to choose in which direction to next sail.

He consider first the direction of the propelling wind. Then he took note of the rising sun. Then . . . to his great surprise, when his eyes looked to the direction the sun would be traveling, he saw overhead, a giant bird. He had only heard about such birds. But, it sudden appearance, when he was considering his next direction, must mean the bird was to be his guide.

So, quickly, he turned his boat to follow the bird, and as he did so, he named his new guide, Aligha. But Aligha was to too fast for Kermicha to keep up with him, even though he paddled furiously. "But thanks anyway, Alligh, I'll follow you in my mind."

Algha's guiding direction must have been good. After several, Kermicha saw that he was approaching a good size island, which he named Samoa. It obviously volcanic, for Kermicha could see fiery smoke rising from its top.

But from as distance, Kermicha, so he was cautious in sliding his boat up on the beach. But suddenly, perhaps it was from the volcanic fumes easing down the distance volcano's side, he felt a little dizzy.

But to his surprise a wonderfully soothing voice entered his mind. "No, young Kermicha, you are not being exfixiated. I have been whispering in your mind to calm you, for you must be thinking clearly to understand what I must tell you, much of which will be disturbing."

The words he was hearing were indeed disturbing, but the soothing voice wouldn't allow him to be disturmbed "Yes, I hear and I understand what you are say. And I am ready to listen to whatever you will tell me. But I can't see you. I believe I would be calmer if your body indeed matched your soothing voice."

Then, slowly a magnificent body came into being halfway up the mountain. And Kermicha felt like he wanted to bolt, but again, the soothing voice kept his still.

The women was indeed maganificant. She was as tall as the talest of trees. And she was drapped in a flowing red dress. And on her head was a gold crown. But even more magnificent was the brilliant fire rising out of that crown.

"Yes, Kermicha, my eager young advertiser, I am the Godless, Lady Volcana, and although I sometimes destroy, I also provide the minerals ashes to enrich the Earth's soil. I do not require you to worship me, though some do, but I do hope you will understand what I must tell you."

Kermicha didn't hesitate, "Yes, I will try hard to understand!"

"This is what I have learned from your mind. You have taken the responsibility of trying to lead your people to a more fertile land, because your Kermadec Island soil is losing its strength to grow enough crops to support your people. I believe that are headed to a group large islands that will provide what you to find.

But this I advise. This island group, which I believe you will name Hawaii, has many fertile self-contained forests and grassland, which will support your people, as long as you keep your population small. But I fear, though your distant descendant population grow so large that a large groups of them will move to settle in another part of the islands. And then the tragedy that I fear will occur will have begun."

Kermicha, although he had tried hard to understand, the new words he was hearing made it difficult. And, in spite of the Godless' soothing voice, he was beginning to worry.

25

But again, the Goddess's voice calmed him, and he was further calmed by what she said next.

"But worry not now, my courage adventurer. It will be many generations before you and your people will have to contend with what I have been telling you. So, fall asleep now, Kermicha. And when you wake, you will just see only a volcano sending forth billows of smoke."

And, in fact, when Kermicha woke, and to his surprise, after a full night's restful sleep, there was only a tall gently smoking volcano . . . and only a vague memory of a troublesom future.

But he *did* remember, so he decided to, yes, worship with a poem.

Goddess Lady Volcano,
Hear my prayer,
I will remember you advice
For I know you do care.
And my people will also worship you,

For that is what appreciative children should do.

Kermicha's mind was still a little fuzzy the next morning, but by continually refreshing his memory, he finally felt certain he knew what had happened. A real goddess had complimented him on his courage and dedication to saving his people. And she had also warned him, and here's where all wasn't totally clear. For a good while his people would thrive. Then, in the distant future, his people would suffer. And it would be centuries before things were better.

But *that* was to be then, and this was good now. Like a competent sailor, he stocked up on water, fruits, and nuts, and set off eagerly on the next step of his journey to save his people.

But, after many days smooth sailing . . . suddenly he felt *something was wrong!* No, he saw something was wrong. He was moving ahead, letting the wind set the course, when overhead he spotted Aligha only slightly above the boat, and sailing along very slowly His bird friend seemed almost casual . . . but no, the way Aligha kept peering back at Kermicha, definitely indicated that Kermicha should be very cautious.

Then Kermicha was certain that that Aligha was worried, the bird rose higher in the air when Kermicha dropped the sail and paddled to a stop.

Moving to the front of the boat, Kermicha stared at the island of Jevis.

There wasn't much to see. It was small flat island, covered mostly with sand, and rocks, and from the smell that came at him, bird manure.

But then there arose perhaps one hundred yards in front the boat arose what appeared to be and oval sandbar, which slowly surfaced, ominously, to become *the head of a giant octopus!*

Kermicha now realized what Aligha was warming him about. And his bird friend was still up above, seemingly shivering with concern.

The the monstrous octopus fully emerge from the water. Its voice along was terrifying, but its size and looming presences was overwhelming. "You have reason to be afraid, little pretend adventurer. I am a sea lord, not that silly little land worm, the cobra. And I am not going sink into the ground and hide from you!"

Kermicha wanted to row his boat forward, and face the octopus, but his rowing arms were paralyzed. But he was able to whisper, "I don't want anything you, Lord Octopus. Please let me sail around you island and be on my way."

"No way, little boy adventurer. If I let you live, you won't be able to lead your people to some mythical new land. So, if I let you live, go back to your Kermadec Island and stop playing big boy sailor."

But what just happened? Did Kermicha see the monster octopus flinch? . . . yes he did. And the beast flinched again, and again. \And then, to Kermicha's enormous relief, he saw, and even felt the heat of Lady Volcano's volcanic ash being sprinkled in increasing amounts on the skin of the octopus.

"Lord Octopus, you are little more than a nuisance to my friend.

So, you had better sink down into your save sea and cool off you sizling"

And the painfully flinching monster did just that. And Kermicha was amused remembering how the cobra had sunk into the earth. I thank you again, Goddess Lady Vocana." And he set hast to sail around Jevis Island. There was nothing there for him. Then, onward he sailed to Kingman Island which from a distances seem almost parklike. Although it had no seanic volcano like he expected to see in Hawaii.

So, eagarly he sailed on expecting to see, as Lady Volcana had promised, the wonderful new homeland to which he was destined to bring his needful people.

But the way was so peaceful, he spent much of that time reviewing his experience with Lady Valcona. He was amused at while the mosters had called boy, Lady Volcana made a point of naming him her young male adventurer. But, to his surprise, he rather liked being thought of a boy by this mothering Goddess. So, he decided to live that role for awhile.

First, after having fun composing, he recited the poem, expecting that the Lady would hear it.

The Good Goddess was in a battle with the Bad Goddess,

And the Bad Goddess struck first.

But Although the Bad Goddess' blow was bad,

The Good Goddess' blow was much worse.

So, the Bad Goddess groveled in the ground,

While the Good Goddess kept her down.

Until the Bad Goddess cried you win.

And then the Good Goddess said.

Don't come back to fight again

Until until the big boy who is reciting this

Is the one who will most likely win.

And as Kermacha fell asleep, he was certain he felt Goddess Volcana nodding her approval.

His next poem occurred to him when this peaceful journey was being interrupted by the threat of rough weather. He was sailing around another island , when this poem came to him.

Brother Lightening struck first,

Quickly followed by his brother, Thunder.

Then Brother Thunder bragged,

I could have seared this little boy

And all you can do is make him flinch.

I agree, said Bother Thunder,

But after he flinches,

His mother will wish he was dead,

Because I made him poop in his bed.

So, Kermacha sailed quickly around Kingman Island, which seemed park-like, but very flat. And he longed for the volcanic mountains the Lady Volcana had promised him.

Again, the way was smooth, and although the breeze was propelling him rapidly, his friend Aligha had flowed quickly ahead, he assumed to await Kermacha's coming to Hahaii.

Kermacha was just waking from a restful sleep, when the bright Eastern sunlight pierced his eyes. And he was almost tempted to close his eyes again because what he had briefly seen was too beautiful to believe, so it must be dream. But nevertheless, he opened his eyes … and what he saw was Paradise. Just ahead of his boat was crystal clear blue water. And further along was bright yellow sand, followed grass so green, it looked edible. Which made since, because it was. Goats were grazing on these salad-greens.

The beyond the grass were a verity of trees, hung will fruits, and nuts and berries, that were unfamiliar to Kermacha. But not apparently to Aligha, who was perched on a tree limb, gouging himself.

So, Kermacha hurriedly beached his boat, and immediately threw himself on the grass, head up, which was fortunate because a large antlered goat was staring in the face.

But Kermacha felt no fear. Maybe it was because the male goat was accompanied by a female mother goat, whose udder was bulging.

Then Kermcha amused himself imagining himself drinking milk, along with a full meal of fruits, nuts, and berries.

Kermacha. But don't kid yourself. Even in your new Paradise, you are too tired. Kermacha sat up, instantly forgot his gourmet fantasy meal, and let his eyes rise up beyond the trees, to the gray slope of a volcanic mountain . . . where Kermacha was certain Lady Volcana was smiling down on him saying, but them laughing, "Enjoy your delicious meal, my big boy, you are to work for your food!

POLYNESIA ENDS EPILOGUE

As the Goddess Lady Volcana explained, Kermicha's Paradisiacal Hawaii did not remain a Paradise for many centuries. As the tribe grew, and groups moved to other parts of the Hawaiian Islands, competition for land, and valuables, and power increased. And by the time the European invasion of the islands began, the many Hawaiian peoples were already at war with one another.

The the European planters, and the Christian ministers, took over the people's lands and tried to delete the Hawaiian people's religion and even their culture.

Fortunately, they were not totally successful. Now, after three hundred more years of this suppression, a successful democratization took place. And Hawaii is now a State, with its own Congress People and Senators, many of whom are of Hawaiian descent, and who are determining how much of the Hawaiian culture will still exist.

In other words, the State of Hawaiians' people, no more than any other Staten's people, can now choose how they want to think, believe, and behave.

Good Luck Hawaiis. I hope that Kermicha would be proud of you.

SUMMARY

As the Goddess Lady Volcana explained, Kermicha's Paradisiacal Hawaii did not remain a Paradise for many centuries. As the tribe grew, and groups moved to other parts of the Hawaiian Islands, competition for land, and valuables, and power increased. And by the time the European invasion of the islands began, the many Hawaiian peoples were already at war with one another.

The European planters, and the Christian ministers, took over the people's lands and tried to delete the Hawaiian people's religion and even their culture.

Fortunately, they were not totally successful. Now, after three hundred more years of this suppression, a successful democratization took place. And Hawaii is now a State, with its own Congress People and Senators, many of whom are of Hawaiian descent, and who are determining how much of the Hawaiian culture will still exist.

In other words, the State of Hawaiians' people, no more than any other Staten's people, can now choose how they want to think, believe, and behave.

Good Luck Hawaii. I hope that Kermicha would be proud of you.

ABOUT THE AUTHOR

D. B. Clark is a retired Clinical Psychologist and college professor who has publish textbooks, novels, and around 90 books of poetry with 40 years of assisting clients become more effective in living. His attempt to manage his own health is documented in his book, *Dr Clark's Health Maintenance Plan*.

Also, read D. B. Clark's daily poems on don-ald71@allpeotry. com where people from all over the world would read and praise his poems.

If you have enjoyed reading this book, you might also like readings these recent books by D. B. Clark: *Forever Young, This Garden Earth, There are My Best Poems of 2019, The Ever Returning Life of Robison Buddy Streets* (Lulu.com) *Poems Promoting Painless Dying* (iUniverse.com) *My Three Favorite Novels* (iUniverse.com).

Printed in the United States
By Bookmasters